STAR WARS®

Jedi Training and Trials
Quiz Book

Random House
New York

© 2002 Lucasfilm Ltd. & ® or TM where indicated. All rights reserved.
Used under authorization. All rights reserved under International and
Pan-American Copyright Conventions. Published in the United States by
Random House, Inc., New York, and simultaneously in Canada by
Random House of Canada Limited, Toronto.
ISBN: 0-375-81602-X

Printed in China   April 2002   10 9 8 7 6 5 4 3 2 1

RANDOM HOUSE and colophon are registered trademarks
of Random House, Inc.

www.randomhouse.com/kids

Official *Star Wars* Web Sites:
www.starwars.com
www.starwarskids.com

ARE YOU READY TO BE TESTED?

You are a student at the Jedi Temple, and how far you progress depends on how much you know. This book is designed to test your knowledge of the Jedi and the galaxy in which they reside. "Training to be a Jedi will not be easy," the venerable Jedi Master Qui-Gon Jinn once said. And he was right!

Remember: Keep your concentration here and now where it belongs, and . . . May the Force be with you!

TEST LEVEL ONE

JEDI HOPEFUL

Welcome to your first test, young hopeful. Many years you have lived here in the Jedi Temple, as long as you can remember. Brought here you were as a baby, when the Jedi found out how Force-sensitive you are. Strong you are in the Force, and much you have learned in your young years.

Studied you have the ways of the Jedi. Meditated you have on the ways of the Force. Know you not firsthand the vast expanse of the galaxy around you, but taught you have been about its cultures and beings. Tested now you will be on what you have learned.

Be mindful! Carefully you must answer these questions. Many Jedi Masters have convened at the Temple. Need apprentices they do. Pass this test you must to become a Padawan apprentice. Then many missions will you be sent on to represent the Jedi and the ways of the Force. Much conflict there is in this galaxy. The Jedi must protect the peace we have upheld for thousands of years.

Your only chance this is to become a Padawan. If pass this test you do not, discover your fate you will at the end of this section. May the Force be with you, young hopeful, or a Padawan you will not become.

JEDI HOPEFUL

10 QUESTIONS (Answer Key at end of section.)

I. GENERAL JEDI KNOWLEDGE

01. What weapon does a Jedi carry?

  __ __ __ __ __ __ __ __ __

02. Who was Qui-Gon Jinn's last Padawan?

  __ __ __ - __ __ __

  __ __ __ __ __ __

03. What all-powerful energy field do the Jedi draw their power from?

  __ __ __   __ __ __ __ __

04. How many members are there usually on the Jedi Council?

    a. 10   **b**. 12   **c**. 9   **d**. 14

05. The Jedi Temple is located on what planet?

    a. Coruscant   **b**. Tatooine

    c. Naboo   **d**. Glee Anselm

06. What young boy did Qui-Gon Jinn find on Tatooine and bring before the Jedi Council?

  __ __ __ __ __ __

  __ __ __ __ __ __ __ __ __

II. JEDI MASTER IDENTIFICATION

IDENTIFY THE FOLLOWING JEDI MASTERS:

07.

08.

__ __ __ __ __   __ __ __

__ __ __ __ __   __ __ __ __

09.

10.

__ __ __ __ __ __   __ __ __ __

__ __ __ __ __

YOUNG HOPEFUL . . .

Discover your fate by turning to the
next page and adding up your answers.
Score one point for every correct answer.

Write your score here _____

A perfect score is 10 points.

If you have scored 6 points or less,
turn to page 10 to learn your fate.

If you have scored 7 points or more,
turn to page 11 to continue your
journey. . . .

ANSWER KEY

JEDI HOPEFUL

I. General Jedi Knowledge

01. Lightsaber
02. Obi-Wan Kenobi
03. The Force
04. (b) 12
05. (a) Coruscant
06. Anakin Skywalker

II. Jedi Master Identification

07. Mace Windu
08. Qui-Gon Jinn
09. Yarael Poof
10. Yoda

JEDI HOPEFUL,

Failed you have to pass our test. To the Agricultural
Corps you will go. To Aduba-3 you are assigned.
A failed mining concern, Aduba-3 is.

Ashamed be not. Many beings there remain, tending
to crops and living in huts on the hillsides.
Poor they are, and in need of help. Maze-stalk
and mizzlegritch moss they grow.

Help them tend these crops you will, and help them defend
their crops against high-hounds you must. Flying beasts,

high-hounds are.
Vicious they are in
their attack on the
crops of these
peaceful
farmers. Help all
they can, the Jedi
must, or several
villages on Aduba-3
will starve.

A farmer will
you now be.

Forever.

TEST LEVEL TWO

JEDI PADAWAN — THE TRIALS

Proven your skills you have, young Padawan. Your Master reports that learned control of the Force you have. Helpful you have been on many missions. Ready you are to face the Trials. If the Trials you do pass, a Jedi Knight you will become. Your own Padawan you will be able to train.

Be mindful, youngling! Becoming a Jedi Knight also means carrying great responsibility. Responsible you will be to uphold the ideals of the Jedi and responsible you will be to protect the galaxy. Strong you are in the Force, but careful you must be or fail the Trials you will. . . .

JEDI PADAWAN — THE TRIALS

50 QUESTIONS (Answer Key at end of section.)

I. GENERAL JEDI KNOWLEDGE

01. When Obi-Wan Kenobi and his Padawan were assigned to protect Senator Amidala, they had just returned from a mission to which planet?

    a. Naboo   b. Ansion
    c. Kamino   d. Tatooine

02. Anakin said he thought his lightsaber skills rivaled Master Yoda's. Did Obi-Wan agree?
    Circle one: YES   NO

03. Anakin's lightsaber color is ___ ___ ___ ___

04. Obi-Wan's lightsaber color is ___ ___ ___ ___

05. Mace Windu's lightsaber color is

    ___ ___ ___ ___ ___ ___

06. Yoda's lightsaber color is ___ ___ ___ ___ ___

07. Was the Kamino system ever in the Jedi archives?
    Circle one: YES   NO

08. Who told Obi-Wan that someone erased the Kamino system from the Jedi archives?
   a. Mace Windu
   b. Jedi Youngling
   c. Shaak Ti
   d. Hermione Bagwa

09. According to Lama Su, which member of the Jedi Council hired the Kaminoans to create a clone army for the Republic?
   a. Yoda
   b. Yaddle
   c. Oppo Rancisis
   d. Sifo-Dyas

10. Qui-Gon Jinn had a Padawan before Obi-Wan Kenobi. What was this Padawan's name?

   ___ ___ ___ ___ ___ ___ ___

11. Obi-Wan Kenobi took Anakin on a mission to this planet to build his first lightsaber.

   ___ ___ ___ ___

12. While building his first lightsaber, Anakin had a vision of

   ___ ___ ___ ___ ___   ___ ___ ___ ___

13. Obi-Wan Kenobi and Anakin Skywalker were protecting Senator Amidala when this bounty hunter tried to assassinate her.

   ___ ___ ___   ___ ___ ___ ___ ___ ___

14. The creatures sent to poison Senator Padmé Amidala when she was on Coruscant are called __ __ __ __ __ __ __

15. After Anakin lost his lightsaber, Obi-Wan Kenobi told him:
   a. "This weapon is your life."
   b. "I'm not paying for another one."
   c. "If you lose your lightsaber again, you are no longer my Padawan."

16. Anakin and Obi-Wan found out that Zam Wesell was a:
   a. Clone   b. Changeling
   c. Wookiee   d. Former Jedi

17. Senator Amidala had been fighting which act in the Senate for over a year?
   a. The Clone Army Act
   b. The Military Creation Act
   c. The Intergalactic Banking Act

18. Jango Fett had never heard of Jedi Master Sifo-Dyas. He claimed he was hired by a man named

   __ __ __ __ __ __ __

19. Name the Representative who granted Supreme Chancellor Palpatine emergency control of the Republic.

   __ __ __ __ __ __

   __ __ __ __ __

20. Senator Amidala and Jar Jar Binks
were members of the
__ __ __ __ __ __ __ __ committee.

21. Jango Fett was paid handsomely to donate his
genetic code for the creation of the clone army.
Other than his fee, he requested only one thing:
   a. A luxurious apartment
   b. A lifetime supply of blue milk
   c. An unaltered clone for himself

22. According to Chancellor Palpatine, the Republic
had been in existence for:
   a. 200 years   b. 500 years
   c. 100 years   d. 1,000 years

23. Mace Windu and Yoda sent Anakin to Naboo with
whom on his first mission?
   a. Obi-Wan Kenobi   b. Senator Amidala
   c. Chancellor Palpatine d. R2-D2

24. Anakin had recurring dreams about this person:

__ __ __ __

__ __ __ __ __ __ __ __ __

25. When Anakin returned to Tatooine, Watto told
him that he no longer owned Anakin's mother.
Who bought Shmi from Watto?
   a. Gardulla the Hutt   b. Cliegg Lars
   c. Ann and Tann Gella   d. Clegg Holdfast

26. Anakin and Padmé found the Lars' homestead. It was located near what spaceport?
    a. Mos Eisley   b. Mos Entha
    c. Mos Espa   d. Mos Bantha

27. Thirty people went out to find Shmi Skywalker. How many came back?
    a. 8   b. 13   c. 4   d. 1

28. What was Shmi doing when the Tusken Raiders kidnapped her?
    a. Watering the plants
    b. Picking mushrooms off moisture vaporators
    c. Laundry

29. Jango and Boba Fett were headed for what planet when they fled Kamino?
    a. Tatooine   b. Geonosis
    c. Naboo   d. Coruscant

30. True or False (circle one): Shmi and Cliegg were married.
    true   false

31. True or False (circle one): C-3PO remembered Padmé and Anakin when they returned to Tatooine.
    true   false

16

II. VEHICLE IDENTIFICATION

IDENTIFY THE FOLLOWING VEHICLES:

32. This vehicle is used by the
    Gungans of Naboo.

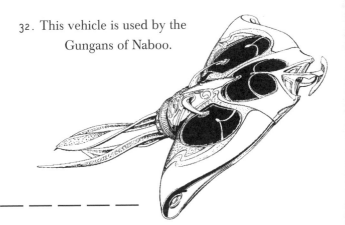

__ __ __ __ __ __

33. This hovering vehicle is used in many parts
    of the galaxy.

__ __ __ __ __ __ __ __

34. This vehicle is used on Coruscant.

__ __ __ __ __ __

35. Jedi use this official vehicle to travel around the galaxy during diplomatic missions.

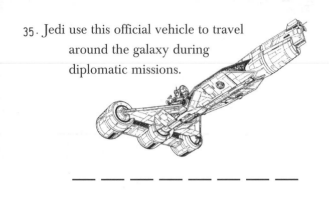

— — — — — — — —

— — — — — — — —

36. The Trade Federation employed this vehicle when invading Naboo.

— — — — — — — —

— — — — — —   — — — —

37. This sleek J-type Nubian vehicle was used by Padmé Amidala when she served as the elected Queen of Naboo. What is this vehicle commonly called?

— — — — —

— — — — — — —

III. ALIEN, CREATURE, AND PLANET IDENTIFICATION

38. Identify this alien's race.

    — — — —

39. Name the planet besides
    Tatooine where the
    dangerous sport of
    Podracing is highly
    popular. It is also
    Sebulba's home planet.

    — — — — — — — —

40. Angels live on the moons of:
    a. Endor   b. Naboo
    c. Ilum   d. Iego

41. Identify the following creature.

    — — — — —   — — — . —

    — — — — — — —

42. Identify the following
    race who scavenge
    for mechanical parts.

—— —— —— ——

43. Identify the race of this
    typical merchant
    on Tatooine.

—— —— —— —— —— —— —— —— ——

44. Nute Gunray is a

—— —— —— —— —— —— —— —— —— ——

45. Name the planet on which the first Clone War battle
    was fought.

—— —— —— —— —— —— —— ——

IV. JEDI MASTER IDENTIFICATION

IDENTIFY THE FOLLOWING JEDI MASTERS:

46. ___

47. ___

48. ___

49. ___

50. ___

a. Yaddle
b. Jocasta Nu
c. Adi Gallia
d. Luminara Unduli
e. Kit Fisto

Discover your fate by looking at the next page and adding up your answers. Score one point for every correct answer.

Write your score here _____

A perfect score is 50 points.

If you have scored 34 points or less, turn to page 24 to learn your fate.

If you have scored 35 points or more, turn to page 25 to continue your journey. . . .

ANSWER KEY

JEDI PADAWAN — THE TRIALS

I. General Jedi Knowledge

01. (b) Ansion
02. No
03. Blue
04. Blue
05. Purple
06. Green
07. Yes
08. (b) Jedi Youngling
09. (d) Sifo-Dyas
10. Xanatos (see **Jedi Apprentice #1**)
11. Ilum (see **Jedi Quest #1**)
12. Darth Maul (see **Jedi Quest #1**)
13. Zam Wesell
14. Kouhuns
15. (a) "This weapon is your life."
16. (b) Changeling
17. (b) The Military Creation Act
18. Tyranus
19. Jar Jar Binks
20. Loyalist
21. (c) An unaltered clone for himself
22. (d) 1,000 years
23. (b) Senator Amidala
24. Shmi Skywalker
25. (b) Cliegg Lars
26. (a) Mos Eisley
27. (c) 4
28. (b) Picking mushrooms off moisture vaporators
29. (b) Geonosis
30. True
31. True

II. Vehicle Identification

32. Bongo
33. Landspeeder
34. Air bus
35. Republic cruiser
36. Armored Attack Tank
37. Royal Starship

III. Alien, Creature, and Planet Identification

38. Gran
39. Malastare
40. (d) Iego
41. Sando aqua monster
42. Jawa
43. Toydarian
44. Neimoidian
45. Geonosis

IV. Jedi Master Identification

46. (e) Kit Fisto
47. (c) Adi Gallia
48. (a) Yaddle
49. (b) Jocasta Nu
50. (d) Luminara Unduli

JEDI PADAWAN,

Disappointed am I in you, young Padawan. Failed the Trials you have. A Jedi must have the deepest commitment to his cause and to the Force, or to the dark side he will fall. Not enough attention have you paid to your studies, and now face the consequences you must.

To your quarters you must go. Meditate you will on the Force while the Council meets to decide your fate. Pleasant it will not be. In your future, clouded though it may be, I see many months striving to capture and relocate Coruscant mutant rats. There, in the Temple's sublevels, you will have long hours to ponder that which you have done.

If lucky you are, the Trials again you will be able to take. *If* lucky you are. Now . . . go.

TEST LEVEL THREE

JEDI KNIGHT

Greetings, Jedi Knight!

Done well you have in training your young Padawan. Passed the Trials to become a Knight your apprentice has. Now *you* are eligible to become a Jedi Master.

Before bestowed upon you this title is, take one more test you must. Disappoint the Council I hope you do not. Concentrate on these questions, answer with care, and a great future you will have in service to the Republic.

JEDI KNIGHT

51 QUESTIONS (Answer Key at end of section.)

I. GENERAL JEDI KNOWLEDGE

01. Name the 12 members of the Jedi Council at the time
    of the Trade Federation blockade of Naboo.
    (This question is worth 12 points, 1 for each
    correct answer.)

a. __ A __ E __ W __ N __ __

b. __ O __ __

c. __ A D D __ __

d. E __ __ __ __ __ O T H

e. __ D __ G __ L __ __ __

f. O __ __ __ __
   __ __ __ C I S __ __

g. Y A __ A E __ __ __ __ __ F

h. D E __ __
   __ __ L L A B __

i. __ V __ N __ __ __ E L L

j. __ I - __ D __ -
   M __ N __ __

k. S __ __ __ __ E E
   __ __ I N

l. __ L O __ __ O O __

02. Identify the external pieces of this
       lightsaber. (This question is worth
       4 points, 1 for each correct answer.)

a. <u>B</u> <u>L</u> __ <u>D</u> __
   <u>E</u> <u>M</u> <u>I</u> __ <u>T</u> __ <u>R</u>
b. <u>A</u> <u>C</u> <u>T</u> __ <u>V</u> __ __ <u>O</u> <u>R</u>

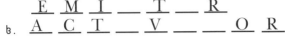

c. __ __ <u>W</u> __ __ __ <u>C</u> <u>E</u> <u>L</u> __
d. <u>C</u> <u>H</u> __ __ <u>G</u> <u>I</u> __ __
   __ <u>O</u> __ <u>T</u>

03. Identify the internal pieces of this lightsaber.
       (This question is worth 3 points, 1 for
       each correct answer.)

a. <u>P</u> <u>R</u> <u>I</u> __ __ <u>R</u> <u>Y</u>
   <u>C</u> <u>R</u> <u>Y</u> __ __ __ __
b. <u>F</u> <u>O</u> __ __ <u>S</u> __ <u>N</u> <u>G</u>
   <u>C</u> <u>R</u> <u>Y</u> __ __ __ __

c. <u>B</u> <u>L</u> <u>A</u> __ __
   __ <u>N</u> <u>E</u> __ <u>R</u> <u>G</u> __
   <u>C</u> <u>H</u> __ __ <u>N</u> <u>N</u> __ __

04. Lightsabers are powered by

___ ___ ___ ___ crystals, named after

the planet where they are found.

05. These crystals are found where on that planet?
     a. Crystal Cave   b. Crystal Mountain
     c. Crystal Lake   d. Crystal Gale

06. Jedi Council member Yaddle is:
     a. 329 years old   b. 477 years old
     c. 201 years old   d. 462 years old

07. Jedi Council member Plo Koon is from the planet

___ ___ ___ ___ ___

08. Jedi Council member Eeth Koth is the same

species as ___ ___ ___ ___ ___

___ ___ ___ ___

09. Did the Jedi Council initially consent to allow
     Qui-Gon Jinn to train Anakin Skywalker?
     Circle one: YES   NO

10. According to Qui-Gon Jinn, Anakin Skywalker was
     the one prophesied to bring

___ ___ ___ ___ ___ ___ ___

to the Force.

11. Count Dooku was once a Jedi Knight.
    According to Ki-Adi-Mundi, Count
    Dooku became:
    a. A murderer   b. A Sith Lord
    c. A political idealist d. A bounty hunter

12. Did the Jedi Council approve the creation
    of a clone army?
    Circle one: YES   NO

13. Qui-Gon Jinn was once taken prisoner by a crazed
    scientist who wanted to learn about the Force.
    This scientist's name was:
    a. Jenna D'Rokrin   b. Genna Ors Phloridan
    c. Zenna Jan Ardor   d. Jenna Zan Arbor

14. Ki-Adi-Mundi is from the planet

    __ __ __ __ __

15. The bounty hunter who captured Qui-Gon
    Jinn and transported him to the above
    scientist was named:
    a. Ona Nobis   b. Zam Wesell
    c. Greedo   d. Jango Fett

16. Obi-Wan Kenobi once left the Jedi Order
    to fight with young idealists on the planet:
    a. Melida/Daan   b. Meluda/Dane
    c. Malisha/Dron   d. Milida/Dain

17. Anakin Skywalker faced his past as a slave
     when he fought the slaver space pirate:
     a. Han Solo   b. Talon Karrde
     c. Krayn   d. Watto

18. True or False (circle one): Jedi are allowed to marry.
     true   false

19. True or False (circle one): Anakin Skywalker
     and Padmé Amidala were married.
     true   false

20. The Queen of Naboo after Padmé stepped down was

     __ __ __ __ __ __ __ __

21. True or False (circle one): According to Master Yoda,
     the battle on Geonosis was a victory.
     true   false

22. Anakin lost what in his lightsaber battle with
     Count Dooku?
          a. A foot   b. His will to live
          c. An arm   d. His Master

23. Which Jedi finally defeated Count Dooku
    on Geonosis, causing him to flee the planet?
    a. Yoda   b. Mace Windu
    c. Ki-Adi-Mundi   d. Obi-Wan Kenobi

24. Who is Count Dooku's current Master?

    ___ ___ ___ ___ ___

    ___ ___ ___ ___ ___ ___ ___

25. Senator Padmé Amidala's Chief of Security was
    named Captain ___ ___ ___ ___ ___

26. Senator Amidala's decoy, who was killed on
    Coruscant, was named ___ ___ ___ ___ ___

27. True or False (circle one): Anakin Skywalker and
    Obi-Wan Kenobi initially agreed that finding
    Senator Padmé Amidala's attacker was implied
    in their orders to protect the Senator.
    true   false

28. Who said the following? "There's always
    a bigger fish."

    ___ ___ ___ - ___ ___ ___

    ___ ___ ___ ___

29. Who said the following? "Fear is the path to the dark side."

    ___ ___ ___ ___

30. True or False (circle one): Obi-Wan Kenobi was the closest thing Anakin ever had to a father.

    true   false

31. According to Count Dooku, Nute Gunray came to him for help after being betrayed by

    ___ ___ ___ ___ ___

    ___ ___ ___ ___ ___ ___ ___

32. Count Dooku was whose Jedi Master?
    a. Eeth Koth
    b. Qui-Gon Jinn
    c. Luminara Unduli
    d. Obi-Wan Kenobi

33. Who saved Padmé from being covered with molten steel in the droid factory on Geonosis?
    a. R2-D2   b. C-3PO
    c. Anakin Skywalker   d. Jango Fett

34. Who are "the lost twenty"?
    a. A notorious band of bounty hunters
    b. Alien refugees from the Outer Rim
    c. The only Jedi who left the Order
    d. A group of Jedi who never returned from a secret mission

II. VEHICLE IDENTIFICATION

IDENTIFY THE FOLLOWING VEHICLES:

35. ___

36. ___

37. ___

38. ___

a. Gondola speeder   b. Republic gunship
c. Republic assault ship   d. Senatorial starship

39. Identify this vehicle and its pilot.
    (Both must be correct or entire answer is wrong.)

Vehicle: ___ ___ ___ ___
___ ___ ___ ___ ___ ___ ___ ___ ___

Pilot: ___ ___ ___ - ___ ___ ___
___ ___ ___ ___ ___ ___

40. Identify this vehicle and its pilot.
    (Both must be correct or entire answer is wrong.)

Vehicle: __ __ __ __ __ __ __

Pilot: __ __ __ __ __ __

41. Identify this vehicle and its pilot.
    (Both must be correct or entire answer is wrong.)

Vehicle: __ __ __ __ __
         __ __ __ __ __ __

Pilot: __ __ __ __ __   __ __ __ __ __ __

42. Identify this vehicle and its pilot.
    (Both must be correct or entire answer is wrong.)

Vehicle: __ __ __ __ __ __ __

Pilot: __ __ __   __ __ __ __ __ __

43. Identify this vehicle and its pilot.

(Both must be correct or entire answer is wrong.)

Vehicle: ___ ___ ___ ___ ___   ___

Pilot: ___ ___ ___ ___ ___   ___ ___ ___ ___

III. ALIEN AND CREATURE IDENTIFICATION

IDENTIFY THE FOLLOWING:

44. The Prime Minister of Kamino, pictured here, is named

___ ___ ___ ___

___ ___

45. This three-horned creature seen in the arena on Geonosis is called the

___ ___ ___ ___

46. This praying mantis–like creature seen in the arena on Geonosis is called the

__ __ __ __ __ __

47. The creatures that attacked Jedi Knight Obi-Wan Kenobi on Geonosis are called

__ __ __ __ __ __ __ __

IV. DROID IDENTIFICATION

IDENTIFY THE FOLLOWING DROIDS:

48. __ __ __ __
    __ __ __ __ __

49. __ __ __ __ __
    __ __ __ __ __ __
    __ __ __ __ __

50. __ __ __ __ __ __
    __ __ __ __ __ __

51. __ __ __ __ __ __ __ __

JEDI KNIGHT...

Discover your fate by looking at the next page and adding up your answers. Score one point for every correct answer.

Write your score here _____
A perfect score is 67 points.

If you have scored 49 points or less, turn to page 40 to learn your fate.

If you have scored 50 points or more, turn to page 41 to continue your journey. . . .

ANSWER KEY

JEDI KNIGHT

I. General Jedi Knowledge

01. (worth 12 points—1 for every correct answer.)
[a] Mace Windu [b] Yoda [c] Yaddle
[d] Eeth Koth [e] Adi Gallia
[f] Oppo Rancisis [g] Yarael Poof
[h] Depa Billaba [i] Even Piell
[j] Ki-Adi-Mundi [k] Saesee Tiin
[l] Plo Koon

02. (worth 4 points—1 for every correct answer.)
[a] Blade emitter
[b] Activator
[c] Power cell
[d] Charging port

03. (worth 3 points—1 for every correct answer.)
[a] Primary crystal
[b] Focusing crystal
[c] Blade energy channel

04. Ilum (see jedi quest #1)
05. [a] Crystal Cave
06. [b] 477 years old
07. Dorin (see episode I visual Dictionary)
08. Darth Maul (see Darth Maul Journal)
09. No
10. Balance
11. [c] A political idealist
12. No
13. [d] Jenna Zan Arbor (see jedi Apprentice #12)
14. Cerea (see episode I visual Dictionary)
15. [a] Ona Nobis (see jedi Apprentice #11)
16. [a] Melida/Daan (see jedi Apprentice #5)

17. [c] Krayn (see jedi quest #1)
18. False
19. True
20. Jamillia
21. False
22. [c] An arm
23. [a] Yoda
24. Darth Sidious
25. Typho
26. Cordé
27. False
28. Qui-Gon Jinn
29. Yoda
30. True
31. Darth Sidious
32. [b] Qui-Gon Jinn
33. [a] R2-D2
34. [c] The only Jedi who left the Order

II. Vehicle Identification

35. [d] Senatorial starship
36. [a] Gondola speeder
37. [c] Republic assault ship
38. [b] Republic gunship
39. Jedi Starfighter, Obi-Wan Kenobi
40. Speeder, Anakin
41. Solar Sailer, Count Dooku
42. Speeder, Zam Wesell
43. *Slave I,* Jango Fett

III. Alien and Creature Identification

44. Lama Su
45. Reek
46. Acklay
47. Massiffs

IV. Droid Identification

48. Pit droid
49. Super battle droid
50. Battle droid
51. Droideka (aka destroyer droid)

JEDI KNIGHT,

For shame! A Jedi Master you shall not become. After being in the Jedi Order for such a lengthy period, know you should the answers to *all* of these questions. Easily you should have been able to answer them!

Though the title of Jedi Knight we cannot take away from you for failing this test, study hard you must to make yourself less ignorant, and punished you must be.

The Council has agreed that for the next year, serve you must on an Ithorian herdship. In the nerf stables you will work, cleaning after them. Spit at you, nerfs will. Meditate hard while tending to these creatures. After this year of labor, again the test you may take.

Do not fail it again–failing twice leads not to pleasant things.

CONGRATULATIONS

JEDI MASTER

Achieved you have the highest level of our Order. Only one honor can you earn beyond this: a seat upon the esteemed Jedi High Council.

Work hard you must to win the respect of your fellow Masters. Years it may take, but as long as our Order exists, a seat in the spire yours someday may be. . . .

THE NEW ORDER

The preceding test is one of the few
artifacts that remain of the old Jedi
Order. It was discovered
on Coruscant after the Empire was
destroyed. We have studied it and
tried to learn all we can of the ways
of old; you must study it, too.

My name is Luke Skywalker. I am
the first of a new generation of Jedi
Knights. You were brought here to the
academy on Yavin 4 because you have
shown yourself to be Force-sensitive. In
order to maintain peace in this fragile
time, I have committed myself to
training young people like you to honor
and respect the Force, using it for the
good of all beings.

THE NEW ORDER

However, before beginning your studies here, you must demonstrate your knowledge of the Rebellion and the events that led to our founding of this Jedi academy. We must not forget our history, or future generations might be subjected to the same tyranny we fought so hard to overcome.

The following test, patterned after the preceding artifact, will examine your knowledge of our history. Remember, you may join us only if you pass it.

Good luck, and may the Force be with you!

THE NEW ORDER

75 QUESTIONS (Answer Key at end of section.)

I. GENERAL JEDI KNOWLEDGE

01. In the cave on Dagobah, Luke Skywalker thought he was confronting Darth Vader. Who was he really confronting?
    - a. Obi-Wan Kenobi
    - b. Himself
    - c. Yoda
    - d. The Emperor

02. Whose son did Obi-Wan begin to instruct in the Jedi ways?
    - a. Yoda's
    - b. Qui-Gon Jinn's
    - c. Mace Windu's
    - d. Anakin Skywalker's

03. Luke Skywalker's first lightsaber originally belonged to:
    - a. Obi-Wan Kenobi
    - b. Qui-Gon Jinn
    - c. Anakin Skywalker
    - d. Kit Fisto

04. What color was Luke Skywalker's first lightsaber?

    — — — —

05. What color was Luke Skywalker's second lightsaber?

    — — — — —

06. When Obi-Wan Kenobi appeared to
    Luke Skywalker on the ice planet Hoth,
    he told Luke to go to:
    a. The Aduba system
    b. The Yavin system
    c. The Alderaan system
    d. The Dagobah system

07. True or False (circle one): Yoda was truthful about
    his identity when he first met Luke Skywalker
    on Dagobah.
    true   false

08. True or False (circle one): Luke was unsuccessful at
    levitating his X-wing out of the Dagobah swamp.
    true   false

09. Luke Skywalker had a vision of the future while
    training with Master Yoda on Dagobah.
    What did he see?
    a. A town in the desert
    b. A village in the mountains
    c. A city in the clouds
    d. A spaceport above Coruscant

    10. According to Yoda, Jedi use the Force for:
        a. Getting what they want
        b. Knowledge and defense
        c. Courage and power

11. What words of advice did Obi-Wan Kenobi have for Luke Skywalker as Luke prepared to save his friends on Bespin?

a. "Don't forget to recharge your lightsaber or you'll be in for a nasty surprise."

b. "Told you, I did. Reckless is he. Now matters are worse."

c. "Don't give in to hate. That leads to the dark side."

d. "Talcum powder will help with the chafing."

12. As the Rebellion celebrated its victory on the forest moon of Endor, Luke was visited by three Jedi spirits: Yoda, Obi-Wan Kenobi, and who?

__ __ __ __ __ __

__ __ __ __ __ __ __ __ __

II. DROID IDENTIFICATION

13. R5-D4, the astromech droid that Uncle Owen bought from the Jawas, blew up because it had a bad

__ __ __ __ __ __ __ __ __

14. C-3PO was afraid that the Jawas were going to send him and R2-D2 to:

a. The moons of Iego

b. The spice mines of Kessel

c. The swamps of Dagobah

d. The Boonta Eve Race

15. The plans R2-D2 carried were for:
    a. The destruction of Alderaan
    b. The Death Star
    c. Darth Vader's TIE fighter
    d. The Rebel base on Yavin 4

16. C-3PO is a:
    a. Cleaning droid   b. Protocol droid
    c. Destroyer droid   d. Death Star droid

17. When C-3PO was first on Cloud City,
    he ran into a very rude droid.
    What type of droid was this?
    a. Protocol droid
    b. Astromech droid
    c. Droid starfighter
    d. Mouse droid

18. True or False (circle one): R2-D2 trusted Yoda from
    the moment he met him.
    true   false

19. True or False (circle one): C-3PO is afraid of nothing.
    true   false

20. True or False (circle one): C-3PO kept his
    comlink on at all times while on the Death Star.
    true   false

21. True or False (circle one): R2-D2 found out that the hyperdrive on the *Millennium Falcon* was deactivated from Cloud City's central computer.

    true   false

22. True or False (circle one): The Ewoks planned to eat R2-D2.

    true   false

23. True or False (circle one): The Ewoks wanted to sacrifice C-3PO to Chewbacca, whom they revered as a god.

    true   false

Name the following droids:

24.

25.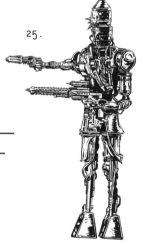

__ __ __ __ __ __

__ __ __ __ __ __

__ __ __

26.

__ __ __ __

__ __ __ __ __

III. HEROES OF THE REBELLION

27. Name the Senator from Alderaan who was on a "diplomatic" mission when Darth Vader boarded her ship.

    __ __ __ __ __ __ __ __

    __ __ __ __

28. Name the young farm boy who found his destiny when Obi-Wan Kenobi retrieved him from the desert.

    __ __ __ __

    __ __ __ __ __ __ __ __ __

29. Obi-Wan Kenobi went in search of a pilot in Mos Eisley. Name the pilot he decided to hire.

    __ __ __   __ __ __ __

30. Name the best friend of the pilot in the previous question.

    __ __ __ __ __ __ __ __

31. Lando Calrissian was promoted to General because of his actions during what battle?
    a. Battle of Hoth   b. Battle of Taanab
    c. Battle of Dantooine   d. Battle of Sullust

32. Name the leader of the Rebellion, who addressed the fleet after the Bothans retrieved plans for the second Death Star.

    __ __ __   __ __ __ __ __ __

33. Name Luke Skywalker's best friend from Tatooine, who died during the attack on the first Death Star.
   a. Biggs Lightdarker
   b. Biggy Smalls
   c. Biggs Darklighter
   d. Biggs O'Deem

34. Who was in charge of the attack on the second Death Star's shield generator on Endor?
   a. Wicket
   b. Logray
   c. Han Solo
   d. Lana

35. Who turned off the tractor beam that was holding the *Millennium Falcon* on the Death Star?
   a. Chewbacca
   b. R2-D2
   c. Princess Leia
   d. Obi-Wan Kenobi

36. The Rebel pilots learned they could destroy the AT-ATs on Hoth using:
   a. Ion cannons
   b. Harpoons and tow cables
   c. Blasters
   d. Proton torpedoes

37. On Cloud City, Han Solo was frozen in carbonite and then given to

    ___ ___ ___ ___   ___ ___ ___ ___

38. Luke Skywalker, Princess Leia, Chewbacca, Lando Calrissian, and the droids went to Tatooine to save Han Solo from:
    a. Zorba the Hutt
    b. Gardulla the Hutt
    c. Priscilla the Hutt
    d. Jabba the Hutt

39. During the Battle of Yavin, Luke Skywalker was:
    a. Red 6   b. Red 2
    c. Red 5   d. Red 9

40. During the Battle of Yavin, Luke Skywalker flew:
    a. An X-wing   b. A Y-wing
    c. A snow speeder   d. A Z-wing

41. Name the pilot who shot a TIE fighter that in turn sent Darth Vader's TIE fighter spiraling out of control during the final run on the Death Star.

    ___ ___ ___   ___ ___ ___ ___

42. True or False (circle one): Princess Leia and Luke Skywalker were actually twins.
    true   false

IV. THE EMPIRE

43. What color was Darth Vader's lightsaber?

     ___ ___ ___

44. True or False (circle one): Darth Vader was the only
    Imperial survivor of the Battle of Yavin.
    true   false

45. True or False (circle one): Grand Moff Tarkin
    wanted to leave the Death Star in his shuttle
    in case the Rebels' plan actually worked.
    true   false

46. How, according to Grand Moff Tarkin, would the
    regional governors maintain direct control
    over their systems after the Emperor dissolved
    the Imperial Senate?
    a. Strict taxation
    b. Police
    c. Fear of the Death Star

47. Princess Leia was a prisoner on the Death Star.
    What level and detention block, according
    to R2-D2, was she kept in?
    a. Level four, detention block AA-thirty-nine
    b. Level six, detention block AC-twenty-one
    c. Level five, detention block AA-twenty-three
    d. Level two, detention block AD-six

48. When Han Solo, Luke Skywalker, and Chewbacca
finally broke into the detention block, Han Solo
found out which cell Princess Leia was in.
Which was it?

    a. 2178   b. 2204

    c. 2362   d. 2187

49. Name the Admiral who thought surprise was the best
idea when the Imperial fleet jumped out of
hyperspace at the Hoth system.

   —— —— —— —— ——

50. True or False (circle one): Darth Vader wanted Luke
Skywalker to join him so they could overthrow
the Emperor.

    true   false

51. True or False (circle one): The Emperor did not want
Luke Skywalker to take Darth Vader's place.

    true   false

52. True or False (circle one): Darth Vader had once
been a great Jedi Knight.

    true   false

53. True or False (circle one): The Empire allowed the
Jedi to remain free throughout the galaxy.

    true   false

54. True or False (circle one): According to Obi-Wan Kenobi, Darth Vader was more machine than man, twisted and evil.

      true   false

55. True or False (circle one): On Cloud City, Darth Vader talked Luke Skywalker into joining him.

      true   false

V. VEHICLE IDENTIFICATION

Identify the following vehicles:

56.

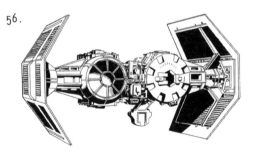

— — — —   — — — — — —

57.

— — ‑ — — —

58.

___ ___ ___

___ ___ ___ ___ ___ ___ ___ ___

59.

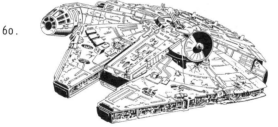

___ ___ ___ ___ ___ ___ ___ ___ ___

60.

___ ___ ___ ___ ___ ___ ___ ___ ___

___ ___ ___ ___ ___

61.

___ _ ___ ___ ___ ___

VI. ALIEN AND CREATURE IDENTIFICATION

62. Jabba the Hutt's palace was on what planet?

    __ __ __ __ __ __ __

63. Greedo, the bounty hunter who tried to capture Han
    Solo in the Mos Eisley cantina, belonged to what
    alien race?

    __ __ __ __ __ __

64. Name the singer in Jabba's palace.

    __ __

    __ __ __ __ __ __ __ __

65. This creature in Jabba's palace attacked Luke
    Skywalker. What was it?
    The __ __ __ __ __ __

66. Jabba told the Rebel heroes that he was going to
    sacrifice them to this creature in the Great Pit
    of Carkoon. What was it called?
    The __ __ __ __ __ __ __

67. Nien Nunb, Lando Calrissian's copilot in the attack
    on the second Death Star, was a member of what
    species?

    __ __ __ __ __ __ __ __ __

68. Bib Fortuna, Jabba the Hutt's majordomo, was a
    member of what species?
    __ __ __ ' __ __ __

69. Name the creatures that sold R2-D2 and
C-3PO to Owen Lars.

__ __ __ __ __

70. Name this alien.

__ __ __ __ __ __ __ __ __
__ __ __ __ __

71. Name this alien.

__ __ __ __ __ __

72. Name this alien.

__ __ __ __ __ __ __

73. Identify this species.

— — — — — — —
— — — — — —

74. The Rebel Alliance used
these creatures as
transportation on Hoth.

— — — — — — — — —

75. This creature ate the
above creatures
on Hoth.

— — — — —

NEW ORDER TEST

You have finished your history test. Turn to the next page to find out exactly how well you did. Each correct answer gives you one point and brings you one step closer to completing your training as a Jedi.

Write your score here _____
A perfect score is 75.

If you scored 59 points or less, turn to page 61 to learn your fate.

If you scored 60 points or more, turn to page 62.

ANSWER KEY

THE NEW ORDER

I. General Jedi Knowledge
01. (b) Himself
02. (d) Anakin Skywalker's
03. (c) Anakin Skywalker
04. Blue
05. Green
06. (d) The Dagobah system
07. False
08. True
09. (c) A city in the clouds
10. (b) Knowledge and defense
11. (c) "Don't give in to hate. That leads to the dark side."
12. Anakin Skywalker

II. Droid Identification
13. Motivator
14. (b) The spice mines of Kessel
15. (b) The Death Star
16. (b) Protocol droid
17. (a) Protocol droid
18. False
19. False
20. False
21. True
22. True
23. False
24. Mark IV patrol droid
25. IG-88
26. R2-D2

III. Heroes of the Rebellion
27. Princess Leia
28. Luke Skywalker
29. Han Solo
30. Chewbacca
31. (b) Battle of Taanab
32. Mon Mothma
33. (c) Biggs Darklighter
34. (c) Han Solo
35. (d) Obi-Wan Kenobi
36. (b) Harpoons and tow cables
37. Boba Fett

38. (d) Jabba the Hutt
39. (c) Red 5
40. (a) An X-wing
41. Han Solo
42. True

IV. The Empire
43. Red
44. False (see Young Jedi Knights: Heirs to the Force—TIE fighter pilot Qorl survived and was living on Yavin 4.)
45. False
46. (c) Fear of the Death Star
47. (c) Level five, detention block AA-twenty-three
48. (d) 2187
49. Ozzel
50. True
51. False
52. True
53. False
54. True
55. False

V. Vehicle Identification
56. TIE Bomber
57. B-wing
58. TIE Advanced X1
59. *Tantive IV*
60. *Millennium Falcon*
61. X-wing

VI. Alien and Creature Identification
62. Tatooine
63. Rodian
64. Sy Snootles
65. Rancor
66. Sarlacc
67. Sullustan
68. Twi'lek
69. Jawas
70. Salacious Crumb
71. Wicket
72. Max Rebo
73. Tusken Raider
74. Tauntauns
75. Wampa

NEW ORDER HOPEFUL,

YOU HAVE SCORED 59 POINTS OR LESS. . . .

It's a good thing you weren't anywhere near our Rebellion, or the Emperor might still be running things!

You need to concentrate on your studies and spend less time dreaming about the future. What's that you say? You seek excitement? Adventure? To quote Master Yoda: "Heh! A Jedi craves not these things!"

You must learn to keep your mind calm and clear, and at peace at all times, otherwise you will open yourself up to the temptation of the dark side of the Force. Now, where would we be if we let that happen?

Go clean up your quarters and write a 4,000-word report about the heroes of the Rebellion.

I want it by tomorrow morning.

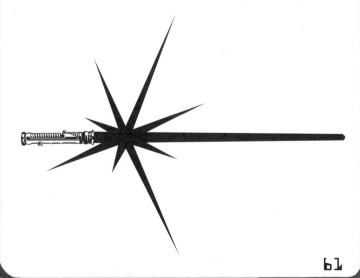

Welcome to the New Jedi Order,
young hopeful.

Let us begin again.

STAR WARS®
ATTACK OF THE CLONES™

Win Hasbro
Star Wars: Attack of the Clones
Holiday Toys . . . in July!

Including action figures, playsets,
electronic figures, and vehicles all before they're in stores!†

Exclusive Offer!

The saga continues with the new *Star Wars* movie, *Attack of the Clones*. Random House is giving you the chance to win all-new *Attack of the Clones* Hasbro toys before they officially hit stores.† Draw a picture of a beloved *Star Wars: Attack of the Clones* character for your chance to win. Some restrictions apply. See official contest rules and eligibility requirements to find out which character to draw and complete details.

Log on to starwars.com for the latest *exclusive* information on *Star Wars: Attack of the Clones*.

www.starwars.com
www.randomhouse.com/kids/starwars
www.starwars.hasbro.com

Win *Star Wars* Action Figures and More!
Official Rules & Regulations

I. HOW TO ENTER
NO PURCHASE NECESSARY. Enter by printing your full name, address, phone number, and date of birth on a piece of paper, and send it to us along with the drawing required for your age group as follows: If you will be at least 5 years old but not yet 9 years old as of June 30, 2002, draw a picture of R2D2. If you will be at least 9 but not yet 12 as of June 30, 2002, draw a picture of Yoda. If you will be at least 12 but not yet 16 as of June 30, 2002, draw a picture of Jango Fett. If you will be at least 16 but not yet 19, draw a picture of Anakin from *Star Wars: Attack of the Clones*. Mail your picture to *Star Wars: Attack of the Clones* Contest, Random House Children's Books Marketing Department, 1540 Broadway, 19th Floor, New York, NY 10036. Entries must be mailed separately and received by Random House no later than June 30, 2002. LIMIT ONE ENTRY PER PERSON. Partially completed or illegible entries will not be accepted. Sponsors are not responsible for lost, late, mutilated, illegible, stolen, postage-due, incomplete, or misdirected entries. All entries become the property of Random House and will not be returned, so please keep a copy for your records.

II. ELIGIBILITY
Contest is open to all legal residents of the United States, excluding the state of Arizona and Puerto Rico, and to legal residents of Canada, excluding the Province of Quebec, who are between the ages of 5 and 18 as of June 30, 2002. All federal, state, and local laws and regulations apply. Void wherever prohibited or restricted by law. Employees of Random House Inc., Lucasfilm Ltd., Hasbro Inc., and their respective parent companies, assigns, subsidiaries or affiliates; advertising, promotion, and fulfillment agencies; and their immediate families and persons living in their household are not eligible to enter this contest.

III. PRIZES
One first place winner in age group 5–8 will win Republic Gunship, 12" Electronic Action Figure Obi-Wan, 12" Electronic Action Figure Jango, Arena Playset, and Deluxe Yoda Figure (approximate retail value $150.00 U.S.) and the winning entry will be eligible to be published in *Star Wars: Attack of the Clones Coloring Book* (on sale fall 2002). One second place winner in age group 5–8 will win Arena Playset and Deluxe Droid Factory with C-3PO (approximate retail value $50.00 U.S.). One third place winner in age group 5–8 will win Deluxe Droid Factory with C-3PO and Basic Action Figure Anakin Skywalker (approximate retail value $16.00 U.S.). One first place winner in age group 9–11 will win Republic Gunship, 12" Electronic Action Figure Obi-Wan, 12" Electronic Action Figure Jango, Arena Playset, and Deluxe Yoda Figure (approximate retail value $150.00 U.S.) and the winning entry will be eligible to be published in *Star Wars: Attack of the Clones Coloring Book* (on sale fall 2002). One second place winner in age group 9–11 will win Arena Playset and Deluxe Droid Factory with C-3PO (approximate retail value $50.00 U.S.). One third place winner in age group 9–11 will win Deluxe Droid Factory with C-3PO and Basic Action Figure Anakin Skywalker (approximate retail value $16.00 U.S.). One first place winner in age group 12–15 will win Republic Gunship, 12" Electronic Action Figure Obi-Wan, 12" Electronic Action Figure Jango, Arena Playset, and Star Wars Unleashed Mace Windu (approximate retail value $155.00 U.S.) and the winning entry will be eligible to be published in *Star Wars: Attack of the Clones Coloring Book* (on sale fall 2002). One second place winner in age group 12–15 will win Arena Playset and Star Wars Unleashed Mace Windu (approximate retail value $55.00 U.S.). One third place winner in age group 12–15 will win Star Wars Unleashed Mace Windu and Basic Action Figure Anakin Skywalker (approximate retail value $21.00 U.S.). One first place winner in age group 16–18 will win Republic Gunship, 12" Electronic Action Figure Obi-Wan, 12" Electronic Action Figure Jango, Arena Playset, and Star Wars Unleashed Mace Windu (approximate retail value $155.00 U.S.) and the winning entry will be eligible to be published in *Star Wars: Attack of the Clones Coloring Book* (on sale fall 2002). One second place winner in age group 16–18 will win Arena Playset and Star Wars Unleashed Mace Windu (approximate retail value $55.00 U.S.). One third place winner in age group 16–18 will win Star Wars Unleashed Mace Windu and Basic Action Figure Anakin Skywalker (approximate retail value $21.00 U.S.). If for any reason a prize is not available or cannot be fulfilled, Random House Inc. reserves the right to substitute a prize of equal or greater value, including—but not limited to—cash equivalent, which is at the complete discretion of Random House Inc. Taxes, if any, are the winner's sole responsibility. Prizes are not transferable and cannot be assigned. No prize or cash substitutes allowed, except at the discretion of the sponsor as set forth above. Random House Inc., Lucasfilm Ltd., and Hasbro Inc. are not responsible if the official on-sale date of the Hasbro toys is moved up to a date earlier than the distribution of the prizes. Names of actual prizes are subject to change. The on-sale date of the *Star Wars: Attack of the Clones Coloring Book* is subject to change.

IV. WINNERS
One first place, one second place, and one third place winner will be selected in each age category on or about July 10, 2002, from all eligible entries received within the entry deadline. Winners will be selected by Random House Children's Books Marketing Department staff on the basis of creativity and originality. By participating, entrants agree to be bound by the official rules and the decision of the judges, which shall be final and binding in all respects. All prizes will be awarded in the name of the winner's parent or legal guardian if winner is under age 18. Each winner and/or winner's parent or legal guardian will be notified by mail and will be required to sign and return affidavit(s) of eligibility and release of liability within 14 days of notification. A noncompliance within that time period or the return of any notification as undeliverable will result in disqualification and the selection of an alternate winner. In the event of any other noncompliance with rules and conditions, prize may be awarded to an alternate winner. Other entry names will NOT be used for subsequent mail solicitation.

V. RESERVATIONS
By entering, winner (and winner's parent/legal guardian) agrees that Random House Inc., Lucasfilm Ltd., Hasbro Inc., and their respective parent companies, assigns, subsidiaries or affiliates, and advertising, promotion, and fulfillment agencies will have no liability whatsoever, and will be held harmless by winner (and winner's parent/legal guardian) for any liability for any injuries, losses, or damages of any kind to person, including death, and property resulting in whole or in part, directly or indirectly, from the acceptance, possession, misuse, or use of the prize, or participation in this contest. By entering the contest each winner, and/or winner's parent or legal guardian as applicable, consents to the use of the winner's name, likeness, and biographical data for publicity and promotional purposes on behalf of Random House Inc. with no additional compensation or further permission (except where prohibited by law). Other entry names will NOT be used for subsequent mail solicitation. For the name of the winners in each age category, available after August 1, 2002, please send a stamped, self-addressed envelope to: *Star Wars: Attack of the Clones* Contest Winner, Random House Children's Books Marketing Department, 1540 Broadway, 19th Floor, New York, NY 10036. Washington and Vermont residents may omit return postage.